QUICKREADS

BLACK WIDOW BEAUTY

ANNE SCHRAFF

QUICKREADS

SERIES 1
Black Widow Beauty
Danger on Ice
Empty Eyes
The Experiment
The Kula'i Street Knights
The Mystery Quilt
No Way to Run
The Ritual
The 75-Cent Son
The Very Bad Dream

SERIES 2
The Accuser
Ben Cody's Treasure
Blackout
The Eye of the Hurricane
The House on the Hill
Look to the Light
Ring of Fear
The Tiger Lily Code
Tug-of-War
The White Room

SERIES 3
The Bad Luck Play
Breaking Point
Death Grip
Fat Boy
No Exit
No Place Like Home
The Plot
Something Dreadful Down Below
Sounds of Terror
The Woman Who Loved a Ghost

SERIES 4
The Barge Ghost
Beasts
Blood and Basketball
Bus 99
The Dark Lady
Dimes to Dollars
Read My Lips
Ruby's Terrible Secret
Student Bodies
Tough Girl

ISBN-13: 978-1-61651-178-4
ISBN-10: 1-61651-178-8
eBook: 978-1-60291-900-6

Printed in Guangzhou, China
0311/03-150-11

15 14 13 12 11 2 3 4 5 6

■ ■ ■

Monique Reed was the prettiest girl Greg Nash had ever seen. When he came to work at the Side Scene clothing store, he couldn't take his eyes off her. He was glad his pal Lew Denison had encouraged him to apply for the job. What a great gig! The Side Scene hired only attractive young salespeople. But Monique was off the charts!

"Hey, Lew," Greg teased, "how come you didn't tell me Miss Universe was working here? Believe me, I would've applied sooner!"

Greg wondered why Lew didn't smile. Usually, Lew had a pretty good sense of humor. "You're talking about Monique? I'd stay away from her, man," Lew said.

"How come? Is she one of those stuck-up kind of girls?" Greg asked.

"No, but I went to high school with Monique. We didn't hang out together that much, but there *were* rumors. Some of the girls at school said that Monique was—well—sort of a witch," Lew said.

Greg laughed. "I bet those chicks were jealous. What girl wouldn't be jealous of Monique?"

"Not the kind of witch who rides a broom," Lew said in a serious voice, "but the kind that can make bad things happen to people."

"Come on, Lew. You don't believe nonsense like that, do you?" Greg asked.

Lew shrugged. "I don't know. The guy Monique was dating a few months ago was killed in a mysterious car accident. He was driving along on a sunny day, and then he just careened off the road into a ditch and was killed! Some of his friends were pretty sure that Monique had something to do with it."

"Ahhh, I feel bad for the poor guy. But

accidents like that happen all the time. He probably fell asleep at the wheel," Greg said.

It was a slow morning at the Side Scene, so Greg decided to wander over to the jewelry counter where Monique worked.

"Hi, Monique. Nice bracelets. I guess the girls really like the brightly colored beads this year," Greg said.

Monique smiled. "Each bracelet sort of does something special for the person who wears it. This rose-colored bead, for example, is supposed to bring you love and romance," she said. Her sweet voice reminded Greg of rich cream dribbling over strawberries.

He picked up a green bracelet and read a tag saying that green beads symbolize wisdom. "Which one is your favorite?" he asked.

Monique smiled and touched the rose-colored bracelet. "This one—because it promises love, of course," she said.

Greg turned to mush. He *had* to take this girl out!

■ ■ ■

Do you like going to the movies?" Greg asked Monique hopefully.

"Actually, I just love country-western music," she said. "I always try to catch a performance when somebody I like comes to town."

Greg loved jazz. He couldn't even name any current country-western music stars. But he smiled broadly and said, "Yeah, I'm into that kind of music, too. Maybe we could go to a concert together sometime."

"I'd like that," Monique said. Then a customer came in and Monique glided away. In a few minutes, she talked a teenaged girl into buying a pair of big hoop earrings.

Between customers, Greg snatched a look at the entertainment section of the newspaper. He found that a local country-western band was playing at a club near the mall. They called themselves the Dust Storm. As he skimmed the brief review, he read that the girl vocalist was supposed to be another Emmylou Harris. Greg had no idea who Emmylou Harris was—but he figured she must be good.

When Monique's customer left, Greg ambled over to her.

"You know, there's a popular little country-western band playing at a local spot tonight. The band is called the Dust Storm. They say the girl singer sounds just like Emmylou Harris. Would you like to go, Monique?" Greg asked.

Monique giggled and said, "Oh, boy, you're a fast worker. Sure, let's go."

Greg's feet were no longer touching the floor as he walked away. He couldn't believe it was so easy to get a date with such a beauty! Sure, he was a good-looking guy, but Monique was *incredible.*

"That gorgeous girl is going out with me tonight," Greg boasted to Lew. "Am I king of the mountain or what?"

"Well," Lew said, smiling faintly, "I hope your life insurance premiums are all paid up."

After work, Greg drove his Acura to Monique's apartment. She shared the place with another girl, Ginger Asinger. The roommate was a nice-looking girl, but Monique put her in the shade.

As Greg waited in the living room for Monique, Ginger sat down to make small talk. "Monique is just nuts about country-western music. I can't get into it myself. I'm into mambo, hip hop—anything but country."

Greg felt the same way, but he nodded and said, "I love country, too."

Then Ginger's smile faded and she turned serious. Her voice took on a "big sister" tone. "Look, Greg, Monique has been through some rough times lately. Her boyfriend got killed a few months ago, and she really freaked—so be extra considerate of her, okay?"

"Sure," Greg was saying just as Monique came into the room. Greg stared. She wore a mauve pullover and jeans in a darker shade of the same color. A golden necklace was around her throat. She looked *magnificent*.

■ ■ ■

"So tell me all about yourself, Greg," Monique said as they drove toward the club. "Do you come from a big family?"

"No, but I do have a brother and a sister," Greg said.

"Me, too," Monique said. "I bet you're the baby, too, just like me."

"Bingo," Greg said with a smile.

"How did your parents treat you—like they *never* really wanted you to grow up and go out on your own?" Monique asked curiously.

"Well, sort of," Greg said. "It's hard to see the last chick fly the nest."

"Is it ever! Mom isn't so bad—but Dad hangs on to me like I'm eleven years old!" Monique complained.

When they parked at the club, Monique got out her wallet and showed Greg pictures of her parents and siblings. There were other pictures, too, pictures of young guys mostly. Were they *all* her boyfriends?

To prepare for this date, Greg had done some reading about country-western music. He wanted to throw some names around—Loretta Lynn, Clint Black, Hank Williams, Garth Brooks—and some of the newer stars like Leanne Rimes.

Monique seemed to be impressed. "Imagine," she cried, "two country music freaks both working at the Side Scene!"

As Greg opened the car door for Monique, he noticed a dark sedan parked on the far end of the lot. What looked like a middle-aged man was sitting behind the wheel. In the dim light, Greg could see the angry scowl on his face.

"Do you know that guy?" Greg asked. "He seems to be glaring at us."

Monique turned her head and sighed. "Oh, I *told* you about my father! I'm twenty-one years old, and he still spies on me! He makes me furious! Sometimes I wish he would just die!" There was a hard edge to her voice.

Watching the dark sedan leave the parking lot, Greg wondered if the man had a screw loose. A father of a young teenager might keep an eye on his daughter while she was out on a date—but not a grown young woman!

"Your father doesn't like you to date *anyone?*" Greg asked.

"I'm telling you, Greg, the man has hated every boy or man who showed any interest in me. He didn't even like my fiancé. When he died a few months ago, my father wouldn't even go to his funeral! I had to stand there by his grave all alone."

"Oh," Greg said. "That must have been the poor guy who lost control of his car and ended up in a ravine."

"I've had enough! I swear I'll call him tomorrow and *demand* that he stop spying on me—or else!" Monique snarled.

■ ■ ■

"Well," Greg thought to himself later that night, "Monique is anything but a witch. I'm surprised she doesn't have some major hangups with such a weird dad, but she's wonderful." Greg knew he had to date her again.

At work on Monday, Greg told Lew what a great time he'd had. "I'm telling you, she's everything I hoped for and then some," he said enthusiastically.

Lew shrugged his shoulders. "Well, don't say I didn't warn you. I met Larry, the guy who ended up with a broken neck in the ravine. Real nice guy. A lot like you, a pretty boy. Charming. Just the type the little Black Widow Beauty likes. You know the story on black widow spiders, don't you? First, the female spider attracts the male spider, and then she kills him."

"Lew, come on—you're just jealous!" Greg laughed.

"No way. I dated her once—but then I decided I value my own neck too much. Fall for Monique, and you'd better start making funeral plans," Lew said.

"Well, then, I'm in no danger, because I'm not a serious kind of guy. I'm going to enjoy being twenty-two and fancy free," Greg said.

The following Saturday, Greg took Monique to the beach. It was a perfect early summer day, and Greg had a great time surfing the mid-sized waves. Although Monique just waded in the surf, she kept a close eye on Greg.

Just before lunchtime, Monique's roommate, Ginger, showed up carrying a picnic basket full of sandwiches and soda. The three of them spread out a beach towel and sat down to eat. They chatted for a few minutes, and then Monique excused herself to go to the ladies' room.

Ginger seemed glad for the opportunity to be alone with Greg. She gave him a big, warm smile. "So, how do you like Monique?" she asked.

"I like her fine," Greg said.

Ginger stared out over the waves for a minute. Then she turned and said, "Monique is so beautiful! When she's around, guys don't even notice other girls. I've been friends with her for a long time. In fact, her fiancé, Larry, was my boyfriend before he started going out with Monique—"

"How come you stayed friends if she took your boyfriend?" Greg asked.

"Oh, she didn't *take* him. He just couldn't resist her. It was clear that he went voluntarily," Ginger said. "But I can't help wondering if he'd still be alive if the two of us had stayed together. . . ."

Greg was astonished by the anger in Ginger's eyes.

■ ■ ■

As Greg finished his sandwich, a wild thought crossed his mind. Was Ginger angry enough to mess with Larry's car? Was it Ginger who caused that fatal tailspin into the ravine?

No, he told himself. That was crazy. Ginger wouldn't do that.

"She's bad luck, you know," Ginger said suddenly.

Pretending ignorance, Greg asked, "Who do you mean?"

"The first one was Rafe," Ginger went

on. "He was a senior in high school when he fell from the roof of the school library. The poor guy went down three stories and *splat*—he hit the ground dead. He was dating Monique then. I was there, Greg. I *know* what happened."

Feeling very uncomfortable, Greg gulped his soda and said, "I guess I'll hit the water again."

"No," Ginger said. "You should hear this. You *need* to hear this. About Pierre, I mean. Monique dated him in college. There was a fire in his apartment and he didn't get out. It was so awful. I went to Rafe's funeral, but I told Monique I couldn't go to Pierre's. She thinks she looks so beautiful in black, and I guess she does. She has several little black dresses just for the funerals—"

"Hey, Ginger, you're freaking me out," Greg said. "Back in the apartment you were telling me to be nice to Monique—that she'd just lost her boyfriend. But now you're hinting that Monique caused all those deaths."

In the distance Greg could hear Monique humming as she walked toward them, her towel slung over her shoulder. But she was still too far away to overhear their conversation.

"I didn't say that Monique was at fault," Ginger said. "I just thought you should know about how her former boyfriends died. I mean—you have the right to know, don't you think?"

"You kinda resent all the attention Monique gets, don't you?" Greg asked.

"Yes, but I'm not telling you this because of that. Desiree, Monique's own sister, said that Monique is a kind of witch. You can ask her. When we were all in high school together, there was this weird aura about Monique. One day a pigeon messed on Monique's new blouse. Monique gave the pigeon the evil eye and that darn bird fell out of the sky, dead!"

Then Monique walked up, looked around, and said, "What's the silence all about?" She turned to her roommate. "You haven't been telling Greg any awful tales, have you?"

Ginger looked down at the sand. "Of course not," she lied, staring at her toes.

Monique looked anxiously at Greg. "No sweat. Everything's cool, babe," Greg said with a big smile.

■ ■ ■

When Greg got back to his apartment, he showered and changed into his pajamas. He watched a little TV and then headed for bed. Within a few minutes he fell fast asleep. It was a warm evening, and the wind blew the curtains through the open window. Greg had chosen an apartment on the first floor of the complex. He didn't want anybody living below him who might be annoyed when he entertained friends or had a party.

Ginger's comments troubled Greg more than he was willing to admit. He slept for half an hour, but then he was wide awake. He wondered—did three guys who dated Monique really die as violently as Ginger said? Or was she just spreading spiteful gossip? It would be a little scary to think that three ex-boyfriends all died in "accidents."

Greg glanced at the clock. It was almost 11:00. Lew Denison was usually up until after midnight. Greg decided to call him and check out Ginger's story. Lew had gone to high school with Monique, so he should know. If some poor dude took a three-story tumble from the school library, Lew wouldn't have forgotten about it.

"Hey, Lew," Greg said, "it's me. How's it going, man?"

"Okay. I'm just playing with the computer, sending some e-mail," Lew said. "So how was your beach date with Monique?"

"It was going great, until her girlfriend—this girl named Ginger—told me a story about a guy named Rafe. I thought you might know if it was true. It sounded off the wall."

"Yeah, it is true. Rafe was in our biology class. They said he took that dive off the roof because he was upset about something—but we all thought that somebody pushed him," Lew said. "Funny thing, though. He was dating Monique at the time. At the funeral she was the picture of grief in her little black dress. Yeah, Rafe's death was a real big deal in our senior year. We dedicated the yearbook to him."

Greg had met Lew Denison two years earlier when he had advertised for a roommate. Then, a year ago, Lew had found his own place. Luckily, Greg was making enough money not to need a roommate. Lew was still a pretty good friend. Greg had never caught him in a lie. "So it's true, then," Greg gulped.

"Sure. What did I tell you? The girl is a Black Widow Beauty. You better run for your life, man!"

"Uh—Ginger mentioned another guy, a French guy in college. You probably wouldn't know about that," Greg said.

"Oh, yeah," Lew said. "Pierre. There was a fire in his place—and he didn't get out." Lew paused a moment and then continued in a strangely quiet voice, "I saw Monique at the funeral. She really does look beautiful in black."

Greg was very unhappy as he climbed back under the covers. But he refused to believe that "black widow" nonsense! Those tragedies just *had* to be awful coincidences.

Greg didn't know how long he'd been sleeping when the smoke alarm went off. He leaped from bed and stumbled through the smoky darkness.

■ ■ ■

The firefighters found kerosene-soaked rags stuffed under the door to Greg's apartment. It was clearly a case of arson. About $1,000 in damage had been done, and smoke had badly discolored one wall. Greg spent two nights in a motel while repairs were being made. But when the arson investigator asked if he had any idea who might have done it, Greg had shrugged and said, "Beats me."

But that wasn't the whole truth. Deep in his heart Greg wondered if Monique was the culprit. But he wasn't about to tell the investigator that. How could he be falling in love with a witch who put curses on her boyfriends?

The following weekend Greg went fishing with his older brother, Dominic. It was a relief to share the whole story with his brother. There was no way Greg could have talked it over with his parents. They would have freaked if they thought he was in danger.

"Seems to me she's not worth it if there's *any* possibility she's some kind of weirdo," Dominic said, as he lowered his line into the lake.

"But, Dom—this is the sweetest, most beautiful girl I ever met!" Greg said. "She's like a dream come true."

"Sounds more like some kind of nightmare to me," Dominic said.

"There's no way in the world this great girl is behind what happened," Greg said. "It's just that she's got a strange roommate, and her dad is real possessive, but—"

"Okay," Dominic said, "so maybe it's *not* her fault. But you're putting yourself in danger, little brother. She might be the best thing since potato chips. But if she's got that kind of baggage, the risk isn't worth it. You hear me?"

Greg stared unhappily into the water. The gloomy gray skies fit his mood. He'd never enjoyed being with a girl as much as he enjoyed dating Monique. Not only was she pretty, she was lively, warm, and fun. He couldn't bear the thought of giving her up.

■ ■ ■

When he and Monique went for a Sunday drive, Greg casually mentioned the fire. "Weirdest thing happened," he said. "Somebody tried to burn down my apartment with me in it."

Monique looked shocked. "Oh, my goodness, no!" she cried.

"Yeah. They stuck kerosene-soaked rags under my door and torched them. Luckily I had a smoke detector," Greg said, studying Monique's face closely.

"Oh, Greg," she whispered, her face distraught, "maybe we shouldn't see each other anymore!"

"Come on, Monique, don't be silly," Greg said. "Why would you say something like that?"

"I—I should have told you before," Monique said in an emotional voice. "I mean about the others." Greg watched giant, pearly tears run down the girl's face. "Some of the boys I dated had bad things happen to them. It's like there's a curse on me or something."

Greg pulled over on the shoulder of the road and put his arm around Monique. "I don't believe in curses," he told her. "If some freak accidents happened to guys you knew, they were just that—accidents."

Monique's big, dark eyes looked stricken. "My own sister said I was a witch. When we were in high school she told everybody that. She said I put curses on people and made terrible things happen to them."

"You're no witch," Greg said. "That's stupid." Then he added, "I bet your sister isn't as pretty as you are. She was probably jealous."

"But Rafe—my boyfriend in my senior year—he fell off a roof and died! And Pierre, this guy I dated in college, he burned up. Then Larry was killed in a terrible car accident." Monique cried harder as she recited the list of horrors. "And now somebody or some*thing* tried to burn *you* up!"

"Monique, look—it's not a spell or anything. But maybe there is some evil person who hates you and wants to hurt the guys you like," Greg said.

Monique's eyes widened in horror. "But who? Who in the world would do such awful things?"

Greg had to be careful. He didn't want to offend Monique by suggesting that a family member or her roommate might be behind the violence. But he had to make his point. "Well, like your sister—maybe she's crazy jealous. Or your roommate, Ginger. Do you think she might—" Greg began.

Monique was shocked. "My *sister?* Desiree? She's my own flesh and blood. She'd never do anything like that. And Ginger is my best friend. We've been best buddies since the second grade!" Monique insisted.

"The other day at the beach she didn't sound like she loved you all that much," Greg said.

"Sometimes she talks too much about the accidents. But she'd never hurt anybody," Monique insisted.

"What about your dad? It was weird how he followed us the other night. Maybe he was trying to scare me off," Greg said.

"My father isn't a criminal!" Monique snapped. Then, in a softer voice, she said, "Oh, Greg, don't you see? I *must* be a jinx! How could anybody risk caring about me? How can *you* risk caring about me? You *do* care about me, don't you Greg?"

Greg pulled Monique closer to console her. As she snuggled into his shoulder, a sly, satisfied look came over her face.

■ ■ ■

By the time Greg headed home, he was exhausted. Still, he just couldn't stop his mind from swirling. He knew it would be smart to just quit the Side Scene and forget about Monique. But he couldn't. He was in love with her. Why, he was even thinking about asking her to marry him!

Instead of going straight home, Greg drove around town for a few hours, trying to clear his mind. First it seemed best to simply drop Monique and get on with his life. But then he pictured her beautiful face, and his resolution crumbled.

When he got home Greg thought a hot shower would be just the thing to calm him down so he could sleep. He went into his bathroom, closed the door, and turned on the shower. Then, as he started to undress, he saw something moving in the corner of the room. To his horror Greg saw the large head of a rattlesnake emerge from the clothes hamper!

The snake slithered from the hamper and positioned itself between Greg and the door. Feeling numb, Greg stood frozen, staring at the creature. He knew that if the reptile detected quick motion, it might very well strike at him.

How could a big rattlesnake have gotten in his bathroom?

When Greg was a Boy Scout, his troop had spotted a rattlesnake while hiking in the foothills. Their leader had said, "That's a western rattlesnake, about six feet long. It's a very dangerous species. Watch out! There's enough venom in that reptile to kill a full-grown man."

There was no doubt that the snake in Greg's bathroom was a rattler. The rattle on its tail and the diamond pattern on its hide were easy to identify.

Greg's heart was pounding hard. He had to get past the snake and out of the bathroom before it became upset and struck out at him.

■ ■ ■

Somebody is out to get me, that's for sure," Greg thought grimly, as he gazed intently at the snake. When it crawled behind the toilet, Greg made his move. He dashed for the door and closed it quickly behind him. Then he ran to the manager's office.

"Somebody put a big rattlesnake in my bathroom!" Greg shouted.

"First a fire and now a rattlesnake!" the manager snarled. "You got some real bad enemies, young fella!"

Animal control soon trapped the snake and took it away. There was no way a rattler could have gotten into the apartment accidentally. All the windows were closed, and the doors were locked. And there were no rattlesnakes in the wild anywhere near Greg's urban apartment complex.

Greg could draw only one conclusion: Somebody was hoping the rattler would fatally bite him.

Greg got in his Acura and headed for Monique's apartment. He had to get to the bottom of this. On the way, he called his friend Lew on the cell phone and told him what had happened. "I freaked, Lew!" Greg said. "A big rattler in my apartment!

Can you imagine?"

Lew responded in a shaky voice. "If it had been dark when you went into the bathroom, you might not have seen the snake in time. I like you, man. I *really* don't want to see you get hurt. Drop the Black Widow Beauty before she makes something *permanent* happen to you!"

Lew's words made Greg angry—so angry that he failed to notice how unusually surprised Monique was to see him at her door.

"Greg!" she cried out in shock. "What—what are you doing back here?" Her phone started ringing, but she ignored it.

Greg started to tell her what had happened. Then a strange thought hit him: *How had Lew known the snake was in his bathroom—unless he put it there?*

"Monique, you dated Lew Denison at one time, didn't you?" he asked.

"Why, yes—just once," she said cautiously. "Why?"

Greg stared at Monique. "Tell me exactly what you thought of him," he demanded.

Monique was quiet for a moment. She seemed to be searching for just the *right* answer. "Well, he wouldn't take 'no' for an answer," Monique said hesitantly. But then she continued with more assurance. "The guy *stalked* me. He was the one who saw Rafe fall off the library roof. And he'd been studying with Pierre just before the fire. And he—offered to change the oil in Larry's car just before the—accident. *Oh, Greg—it has to be Lew!*"

"I'm sure you're right, Monique. I'm going to Lew's right now. You call the police. Have them meet me there."

As soon as Greg left, Monique punched in Lew's phone number. Lew's voice was frantic. "Monique, I've been trying to reach you. Greg is . . ."

Monique interrupted in a hard voice. "Well, you've messed things up good, Lew. Greg's on his way to your place right now. Finish it right this time!" she yelled. "Finish *him!*"

Then Monique's voice became soft and

luring. "Come on, Lew. It's been so long since I wore black. And you know just how good I look in black. . . ."

After-Reading Wrap-Up

1. Outline the plot of *Black Widow Beauty* in three or four sentences. In the first sentence, identify the unsolved mystery. In the following sentences, tell how the mystery was finally worked out.

2. Write two sentences describing each main character: Monique, Greg, and Lew.

3. When you learned the truth about Lew, did you feel sorry for him? Explain your thinking.

4. Who do you think was the most interesting character in the book? Why?

5. In the end—when you discovered the truth about Monique and Lew—were you surprised? Explain why or why not.